FOR
RIPLEY

Copyright © 2013 Pranas T. Naujokaitis
Balloon Toons® is a registered
trademark of Harriet Ziefert, Inc.
All rights reserved/CIP data is available.
Published in the United States 2013 by
🍎 Blue Apple Books
515 Valley Street, Maplewood, NJ 07040
www.blueapplebooks.com

First Edition
Printed in China 04/13
ISBN: 978-1-60905-296-6
2 4 6 8 10 9 7 5 3 1

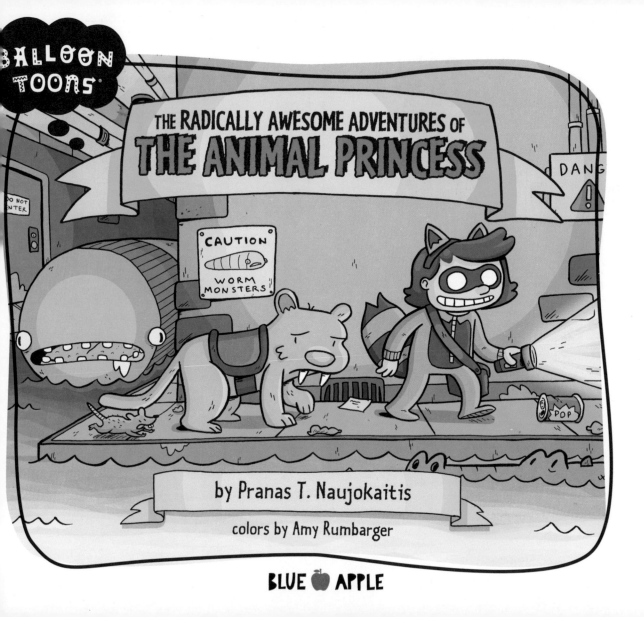